THE

PRODIGALS

Book 4 in the *"Stay in the Castle"* Series

By Pastor Jerry Ross

To order additional copies:

www.stayinthecastle.com

or call (812) 665-4375

Introduction

The name *Angus* means "one choice." We were introduced to him in *The Warrior Prince*, the second book of the *Stay in the Castle* series.

I was amazed at the emotional reaction from my readers to this secondary character. One wrote, "The one scene in *The Warrior Prince* that brought me to tears was Angus' homecoming. I'm a parent who still watches from the ramparts." Another wrote, "Thanks for getting the older brother home. I am Angus."

In this story, you will also meet Willow, the prodigal princess. She was the once nameless young lady in the original *Stay in the Castle* booklet.

I have a dozen reasons why their stories needed to be written, and only one reason why I hesitated — I do not want to plant in any young person's mind the thought that it is OK to miss God's best will — God's perfect will. You will notice Angus walks with a limp and Willow carries her own inward scars. There is always a cost when you leave the King's Castle or forsake the King's Highway — and no guarantee that you'll ever get back.

But I also want to give hope to those who may have been deceived by the dragon. You can come home. The Father still loves you — the King still has a plan for your life. God's second best is still a thousand times better than anything this world can offer.

One wrong choice can get a life off track. One right choice can put it back on track. If this helps get one Angus home or one princess back to the castle, then it is a worthy project.

— *Jerry Ross*

I have gone astray like a lost sheep;
seek thy servant;
for I do not forget thy commandments.
Psalms 119:176

The Castle Wedding

"I'm telling you, we have to stop this wedding!"

Jozy huddled with his castle gang, a group of five to seven-year -old orphans who lived in the King's castle, ate the King's food, learned their letters, ciphered numbers, did chores, memorized their verses from the *Book of Lessons* — but the rest of the time ran and wrestled and pretended and played. Today's secret meeting had been called by Jozy and was being held in the hay loft of the barn that housed the King's war stallions.

"Stop the wedding? Have you lost your mind?" The boy who spoke was blond-headed and scarecrow thin. He had been found by the King — actually caught by the King — as he was trying to steal food from one of the castle supply wagons. Everyone called him Jangle, because of his one prize possession — a single bell he found along the road that must have come loose from a horse's harness but now hung by a cord around his neck. It made a pleasant sound, but tended to get you caught when you were trying to steal food. Thanks to the King, he didn't have to worry about being hungry anymore.

Four other orphans — Rooster, Dizzy, Oatcake and Fleabite — all looked at Jozy like he had been dropped on his head. Each one had been abandoned due to neglect or misfortune, adopted by the King and brought to the castle. They were as thick as thieves and closer than blood brothers.

Jozy pressed on, "I've been thinking on this for a week. If we all work together, I think we can kidnap Vala. Then Prince Rinc would have to find some other girl to marry."

"Kidnap Vala? You have lost your mind!" Dizzy stared at him — well, with his good eye — in disbelief. His other eye always looked off to the left a bit, giving the impression that he was not only looking at you, but also for anyone who might be sneaking up on you.

Fleabite scratched at an itch. "I can tell you right now, boys, Prince Rinc is not going to marry anyone but Princess Vala. He gets all starry-eyed just looking at her. You try and kidnap her, and Prince Rinc will hang you by your feet off the castle ramparts for a week."

Oatcake reached into his shirt and pulled out a large biscuit, one he had smuggled out of the castle kitchen. He bit off a big chunk, then talked his chewy talk. "What do you have against Prince Rinc? Didn't he save you from getting slaughtered or something?"

Prince Rinc had rescued Jozy, his twin Gemma, and older siblings Twain and Risa, from a wicked murderer back when they lived in the dark village. Twain, almost thirteen, was being trained to be a warrior. Risa, now eleven, served in the kitchen and was already famous for her pastries and cakes. Oatcake was secretly in love with her.

"I don't have anything against him. But if they get married, then he is going to take her to the dark part of the kingdom, to erect a new castle and battle the evil there. If that happens, we'll never see her again. So we have to kidnap her."

This gave everyone pause, all lost in their private thoughts of Princess Vala. She was one of the young women who oversaw the children, and she was everyone's favorite — tough when she needed to be, but mostly sweet and kind. The castle gang loved Vala and it would break their hearts to see her go.

Rooster, his red hair sticking straight up as if his Creator had commanded it to stand at attention, stubbornly shook his head. "Well, you better come up with a better plan if you want to stop this wedding. 'Cause we only have a week, and we'll never get away with kidnapping Princess Vala."

They all leaned back into the hay, pondering fiercely, determined to come up with the perfect plan.

****

Vala paced the floor of her bedroom, stopping now and again to reexamine herself in the reflecting glass. Risa sat on Vala's bed, brushing spotless the princess's satin shoes.

Risa glanced up and noticed Vala's critical self-examination and furrowed brow. "Vala, you look wonderful! Don't be nervous, Prince Rinc's family is going to love you. How could they not?"

Vala came over and sat on the bed beside her. "He speaks so highly of them. His father is a famous lord, and his mother — well, he adores her. Everything he tells me about her — such a lady, and oh so wise..." She stared off, the furrows deepening.

"And if she is 'oh so wise,' then she will immediately know how special you are!"

"Risa, it's more complicated than that. He was raised in a castle, I was raised in a shack in the mountains. When he turned twelve, he started preparing to be a prince — I turned twelve as a slave girl scrubbing floors for my wicked aunt. He's a prince, and I'm..."

"...the most amazing princess in the kingdom!" Risa interrupted. "Vala, remember what you told me during our long night talk?" Risa always called it that — the night, two years ago, Vala had told her and Twain the tale of her life. "I told you that night that I wanted to grow up and be you. And you said that I was going to be something better than you — I was going to be *me*, the one and only *me*."

Vala smiled at the memory of that night.

"Well, there is only one Vala, and I don't care what you once were, I know who you are now. And who you are now is who Prince Rinc fell in love with. And his father and mother will also."

Vala reached out and gave her a mighty squeeze. "Thanks, Risa, I needed to hear that. Now tell me of Twain. I see so little of him since he began his warrior training."

"Prince Rinc marvels at his quickness and skill. Twain is not only mastering the sword, he has a cunning about him — an ability to read other men and find their weakness. Away from the training field, Twain is soft spoken, but when he puts on his armor and takes up his weapons, he is fierce and relentless."

Vala nodded. She had always known he would make a mighty warrior. She was so proud of how Twain and Risa had progressed since arriving here almost three years ago. "You should be proud of him. He will be a great asset for the King. Risa, I also love who you are becoming. The castle cooks say you are gifted — that you could take water and rocks and cook up a savory stew!"

Risa laughed. "I do love to cook and bake. Mostly because I love watching people enjoy it so. The cooks are too kind. I would know nothing about baking if they had not taught me, and nothing about being a lady if it were not for you."

"Soon you will blossom into a beautiful young woman."

"I do long for it. It seems growing up takes forever!"

Vala reached out and took her hand. "It will all come faster than you think. Seems I just arrived here and now I'm a week away from being Rinc's bride. If you would have met me when I first escaped Turpis Villa — I looked the most unlikely princess."

"I don't believe that," Risa said and meant.

Vala grimaced at the memory. "It's true. The day I first arrived at the kind lord's castle, I was a mess! Popped up out of a load of hay, smuggled out of the dark kingdom with a price on my head. No manners, no proper upbringing, and my only examples for womanhood were my poor mountain mother — then after she died, Thira, Atgas, and the porch women!"

"But you are so perfect now. If that is really what you were, how did you become such a lady? Who helped you become... you?"

"Who taught me?" Vala looked down at her folded hands, then out her bedroom window at the village below. "The most wonderful princess who has ever graced this castle."

Willow

The castle lord sized me up as I stood before him — hay still strawed my hair, wrinkled servant's dress, dirt-streaked, disheveled, and exhausted. All I could feel was a great sadness trapped within me. The lord stared hard, skeptical that I could really be the most wanted person in the kingdom. Ubel had placed a price on my head — a helmet full of gold for information of my whereabouts.

The kind lord spoke honestly. "I fear for your safety, even in this strong castle. Ubel's power are far reaching in this region of the kingdom, and sooner or later, word will get out that you are here. Because of this, I need to get you to the King's castle as soon as possible."

He accomplished this by sending me with four of his trusted warriors, all of us dressed as peasants, using only the hidden mountain trails. My bodyguards worried that I would not be strong enough to endure the rock strewn trails and peaked passes, but they worried for naught — my mountain upbringing gave me billy-goat stamina. Still, the journey took the better part of three weeks.

When I peaked the last pass and looked down at the King's castle, I wept. My protectors did not know of Adeen and her stories — stories I thought she created from her rainbow-colored imagination. Yet all that she told me was true: there was a King, and he did take in orphans. With all my heart, I wished she was standing here with me.

"She died so I could live," I said out loud.

"Pardon, Missy?" one of the warriors offered.

I looked at him, then away, not answering. Adeen's death had bought me two days without pursuit. Ubel assumed I lay dead with Adeen at the bottom of the rocky gorge. Without that head start — without Adeen's sacrifice — I would now be Ubel's prisoner.

A trumpet sounded and soldiers rode out of the King's gate, extra horses saddled and in tow, up to where we waited. Minutes later, I was riding through the gate of the castle.

As I entered the courtyard, two people stood waiting — the Great King and his favored daughter, Willow.

****

Vala sighed, "You should have seen her. Willow was the choicest of all the King's daughters. Yes, she was striking in her appearance, but that is not what you first noticed. There was something else — a spirit, an anointing — it is hard to describe."

Risa smiled. "You don't have to — I see the same in you."

Vala blushed a smile, "I was just shy of turning fifteen and Willow was seventeen. The King put me in her care, and my life was never again to be the same. You asked what turned me into a princess? Two things — the King's love and Willow's friendship."

"I can't wait to meet her! Did she marry a warrior prince or a castle lord? When will she arrive for the wedding?"

Vala reached out a finger and flipped a strawberry curl out of Risa's face, tucking it behind her ear. "She's not coming."

"But, why not?"

"Risa, I would love nothing more than for Willow to be here on my wedding day. But she won't come. You see, she made a mistake — the greatest mistake a princess can make. Willow decided, a few years ago, not to stay in the castle."

****

For the next three years, Willow and I were inseparable. She had been brought to the castle when she was four years of age and, because of that, she had no clear memories of village life. This was a blessing, but also proved a danger.

Willow saw something romantic in my past life — from my mountain upbringing to my time at Turpis Villa, Willow wanted every detail. I told her of the evil, and she listened, but looking back now, I wonder if she really comprehended it.

I learned so much from Willow. She had a very special relationship with the King — there was such a genuine love between them. Willow excelled above all in her princess training, her graceful skills, and her memorization of the *Book of Lessons*. I wondered at her ability to remember the passages so clearly. She told me once that when she looked at a page of the *Book*, her mind made a portrait of it — that she could close her eyes and see the page. I tried to do the same a dozen times but I didn't have that gift.

Outwardly, Willow was the perfect princess. But at times I would find her in the middle of the night, leaning out her window, looking and listening toward the village below. On rare nights when the wind would come from the southeast, you could hear the village music and merry-making. For Willow, there was a curiosity about it that none of us who had firm memories of our village days possessed.

The King sensed Willow's restlessness and curiosity. He explained to her many times that if she were patient — if she stayed in the castle — then in time, the right prince would come for her. Willow would be content in this knowledge for months at a time, then she would be drawn to the village again.

Then, one evening, the dragon set his trap. She was alone in the kitchen when one of the village delivery boys chanced by. He filled her head with romantic tales and painted the village life in pretend colors. The Fall Festival was starting, and he enticed her into sneaking out of the castle to join the festivities for just one evening — just one.

Sadly, she gave in to the temptation. One night turned into many more and soon, she lost her heart to this village lad. As soon as I saw what was happening, I went to the King and told him all I knew. He tried several times to talk to Willow, pleaded with her to be patient and wait for the perfect time — to wait for the chosen one. But sadly, her heart was fixed, and a few months later, she left the castle to marry the dragon's counterfeit.

I have never seen the King so broken. He had purchased her from a cruel master, provided her every need, treated her like his own daughter and made her into a princess. The night she left, I went to him and wept on his shoulder. He whispered in my ear, "Vala, this castle is not a prison, it is a decision. Willow chose the world over the will of her King. You too, one day, must choose. Remember this night, and vow now to do right."

As I wept into his chest, I swear I could hear his heart breaking.

****

Risa now was in tears. She sat and imagined how devastated she would be if Vala made such a choice. "I am so sorry. Do you think... if she knew you were getting married, that she might consider coming?"

"I sent one of the servants to deliver an invitation. I included a handwritten note, asking her to come. She told the messenger that she was glad for me, but would not be attending. I think she is too ashamed of what her life has become."

"How bad is it?"

"Her husband left her for another woman about a year ago. She struggles to raise her three year-old daughter, a sweet little girl she named Lola. Willow tends her garden, sells her vegetables, takes in laundry — whatever she has to do to survive. The King has offered to help, but she is proud."

Vala folded her hands into her lap, struggling with her emotions. "Risa, my wedding day will be the happiest day of my life. I will feel only two sorrows on that day — the sadness that Willow will not share it with me, and my failure to keep my promise to Adeen."

"What promise?"

"To rescue Pem. Rinc has promised me that we will try to free Pem after we establish a castle stronghold in the dark part of the kingdom, but I worry about her every day and fear the horrors she endures." Vala took Risa by the hand. "I have been so blessed, and I don't want to sound unthankful, but I would give anything to have Willow and Pem here on my special day."

Risa stared off into the distance, thinking. She could not bear to see Vala unhappy.

****

Jozy stood and called the barn loft meeting to order. "I've got it! I know how to stop the wedding."

Dizzy stared hard, both at him and left of him. "No more fool talk of kidnapping Vala. You're going to get us punished again."

"Last time we followed one of your tortoise-brain schemes, we all got sent to bed without our supper." Oatcake gripped his protruding stomach at the memory. "I almost died of starvation that night!"

"Just hear me out. This will work and they will never know who did it. I've been talking to Risa — she keeps going on and on about this wedding."

Rooster nodded, his red comb bobbing. "Weddings turn girls into giddy, giggling hyenas."

"Anyway, Risa keeps going on about Vala's beautiful white wedding dress. So I asked her, 'Why does she have to have a special dress to get married in?' And Risa says, 'You have to have a wedding dress. A princess can't get married without a white wedding dress!'"

"I see!" interrupted Fleabite. "If we steal the wedding dress, then no wedding!"

Jozy glared at him, angry he stole his thunder. "That's what I was getting at. All we have to do is wait till the morning of her wedding, sneak into her room, steal her wedding dress and hide it here in the barn. Then Vala can't get married, and she will have to stay here and take care of us."

"I don't know..." Oatcake pondered, still patting his stomach.

"Well, do any of you have a better idea? You know how good we have it with Vala watching us. What if she leaves and Princess Henny is put in charge? How much fun will we have then?" That argument erased whatever objections might have remained. Henny was a slightly plump, sweet princess, but when it came to little boys, she was only happy when they were busy studying or doing chores.

Jangle sprang to his feet, his bell tinkling. "I make a motion we steal the dress!" The rest jumped to their feet and began to cheer.

They had their first real warrior mission!

Wedding Guests

The entire castle population turned out for the arrival of Prince Rinc's family. A shout went up as they rode through the castle gate — his parents, Lord Callan and Lady Ava, leading the procession. Following behind were Rinc's three younger sisters — Clarity, Grace, and Everjoy — and bringing up the rear, wearing a wide ear-to-ear grin, his older brother, Angus. Behind the family rode Lord Callan's castle warriors, twenty strong.

The next several minutes were spent in sweet, tearful reunion — father's formal handshake, then strong embrace followed by a mother's hug that lasted long. Rinc then swept up all three of his sisters in one huge embrace, twirling them together off their feet.

"What happened to my little sisters? I left you as little girls and you come to me as beautiful young women!" They giggled and blushed — three blossoming princesses: sixteen, fifteen and twelve. All three adored their warrior prince brother.

Finally, he stood before Angus, each giving the other a warrior's stare. Then they laughed and embraced, each trying to squeeze the life out of the other.

Rinc held Angus at arm's length, taking stock. Angus was always a bear of a man, jolly in nature and strong as Samson. His three prodigal years had left him physically weak and spiritually sapped — it had also left him with a slight limp — but two years back home had transformed him into his old self once again. "You look fit, my brother. It is so good to see you."

"It took several months to regain my strength and retrain my sword skills, but now I lead the castle guard back home."

Rinc smiled. "You were always the better warrior. It is good to have you back."

"Yes, and you have always been the younger brother. Don't ever forget that." Each loved the other, each had saved the other, and their bond would be forever strong.

The entire family then made their way to the King, giving him reverence and receiving from him kind words. Then all turned to the palace door to see Vala make her way nervously toward the family.

Rinc stepped forward to escort her. "Father, Mother, this is my bride-to-be. This is Vala." She curtsied, then smiled, a blush coloring her cheeks. Lord Callan stepped forward, taking the hand she offered. He looked into her eyes, so seriously, then followed it with a charming smile and a wink. It made her laugh. She was so nervous that she broke protocol, reaching up and hugging his neck. Rinc saw that it delighted his father.

Rinc's sisters came next, hugging and talking all at once until finally Angus came to her rescue, scattering the girls, bowing, and kissing her hand.

"I have no idea what you see in my donkey of a little brother, but I'm glad you took pity on him and agreed to marry him." He then laughed at his own joke, happy for them both.

Rinc's mother stood a few yards away, taking in the scene. Vala looked into her eyes, wondering what she was thinking. Lady Ava glided toward her, then reached out and took both her hands. She spoke quietly, so that only the two of them could hear.

"I understand that your parents were tragically killed when you were young — that you were orphaned." Vala stared into her eyes, so frightened, not understanding her meaning — then slowly nodded a yes. "From this day forward, if it pleases you, I would love to be your mother, and my husband, your father. I have prayed for you since my son was born — every day — that God would keep you and bring you to him. So, if this pleases you, from this day forward, we would love for you to consider us your family. Would agree to be our daughter?"

Vala had never felt so loved — so wanted. A tear spilled from each eye. "Lady Ava, nothing would please me more." The two embraced, and the crowd cheered. Lady Ava waved everyone to silence. "The servants will see to our things, and Rinc, you take care of settling the family. Vala and I have things to talk about." And with that, she hooked her arm into Vala's and the two walked toward the courtyard to discuss things that mothers and daughters do at times like this.

****

The lord and his two warrior sons met privately upon the ramparts. Rinc told Vala's life story — of her friend, Pem, and Vala's promise to Adeen to one day rescue her. He then spoke of Ubel's thirst for revenge, and the price still offered for Vala's capture.

Rinc then reported the evidence he had found, months earlier, left by the mysterious spy who had been watching the castle from the distant forest. Angus stared towards the west, anger in his eyes. He then asked his father, "Do you think Ubel is a real threat?"

Lord Callan nodded. "I have heard of Ubel. Ten years ago, he was just another lowly dark lord, but his cunning and ruthlessness have elevated his status and power. Yes, if Ubel feels he has been offended, his pride will drive him to seek revenge."

"Will he try to disrupt the wedding?"

They waited for their father's opinion. "I think he will use cunning instead of a direct attack. The King's castle guard is the best in the kingdom. Our warriors strengthen his defenses by twenty. We must be vigilant, but no, I doubt he will try a direct attack. Be sure of one thing — he has men in the village below, spies all around. We must be vigilant."

Rinc balled his hands to fists. "If anything happens to her…"

Angus interrupted, "No worries there, little brother. She will be protected. On my life."

Lord Callan looked at his two sons, and when he spoke, there was iron in his words. "Ubel has spread much destruction and sorrow. Sooner or later, all his evil will catch up with him. I pray that I am there when it happens."

All three, now of one mind, stared out into the darkness.

The Wedding Day

After breakfast, Risa found Jozy and his castle gang hidden in the hay loft, sitting in a circle whispering secrets. As she climbed into the loft, she heard them grow quiet.

"No girls allowed!" Jozy snarled, upset by Risa's interruption.

"I need your help — all of you."

They looked at each other, conflicted. They had an important mission planned, one that had to be carried out before the afternoon wedding — a wedding dress needed to be kidnapped. But then again, Risa usually had little time for Jozy and his friends. The fact that she needed them made them feel important.

"You need us?" Dizzy said as he looked at everyone in the circle twice, once with each eye.

Oatcake was entranced. "Anything, just name it."

She quickly retold a short version of Willow's story. "Vala should have no sorrow on this day. We can't rescue Pem, but if Willow attending the wedding will make Vala happy, then I have to try to convince her to come. It would be my gift to Vala — our gift to Vala."

Fleabite picked at a scab on his big toe, then blurted out, "What if the wedding doesn't happen at all?" Rooster gave him a kick in his shin as the others glared his way.

Risa looked puzzled. "Well, why wouldn't it?"

Jozy quickly distracted her. "What do you need us to do? We'll do it, as long as it doesn't take too long."

Risa sat down in the circle and told them her plan.

****

The wedding was planned to begin an hour after high noon, now just two hours away. The castle buzzed with last minute preparations, the courtyard decorated for the occasion. The smell of fragrant fruits, baked bread and smoked meats filled the air as the after-wedding feast was prepared. Lords and ladies arrived from distant castles, each escorted by family members and friends. This was a day no one in the kingdom wished to miss.

Extra warriors had been stationed around the castle perimeter to dissuade the King's enemies from disrupting the ceremony. Seven castle guards watched the small wooden bridge that led from the castle grounds to the village below. All seven were at attention, all with shining swords and iron-studded shields, all eyes watching the village.

Then, from their left, six warriors rose from a small wrinkle in the landscape, swords drawn, bellowed their warrior cry, and attacked.

****

It took Jozy, the castle gang, and Risa over an hour to slither down to the warriors guarding the bridge. Because of a slight run-off ditch that ran down from the castle — and their small size — they were able to accomplish it undetected. Their wooden swords and makeshift armor were dragged along with them.

Jangle had been made to leave his bell in the club house, but he was not happy about it. Finally, to get him to agree, they told him he could lead the charge. When they were all in position — swords ready, leather hats for helmets, board shields firmly gripped — Jangle whispered one last instruction.

"Ok, men, when I count to three, we attack."

Jozy, still sore that he wasn't leading the charge, added, "And don't forget that we have to loop around and draw their attention away from the ditch."

Jangle hissed, "I know what I'm doing! We've gone over this a hundred times."

Oatcake was still breathing heavily. He had never crawled this far before and wanted to go back halfway there, but Risa's promise of a whole plate of pastries for breakfast in the morning drove him on. Now he was glad he came, caught up in the excitement of the moment. "Do we take any prisoners or do we slaughter the lot of them?"

Dizzy rolled his eyes, the left chasing the right. "We pray we don't get slaughtered."

Risa hissed, "Come on, boys. This is for Vala. Time to go."

Jangle nodded. Six little boys' faces took on warrior determination. "One, two… THREE!"

They sprang up and ran in a loop, above the sentries, screaming a battle cry. Then, they changed direction, and charged.

****

The second the boys screamed their attack, seven trained castle warriors unsheathed their swords, whirled toward them, and formed a shield wall. When they identified their would-be attackers, laughter rose from their ranks. It increased in intensity, as they watched the boys loop around them, and then attack from the opposite direction.

The commander, enjoying the entertainment this provided his men, smiled, then barked, "Lock shields! Rule number one, lads — never underestimate the enemy."

As the six closed the distance, Dizzy followed the wrong eye and ran left into Oatcake. Their feet tangled and they fell hard in a heap ten yards from the warriors. Several soldiers were laughing so hard they lowered their shields.

Jozy — determined to seize the advantage — yelled, "There's a break in the shield wall, follow me!" The remaining four, wooden swords raised, charged into the gap.

The warriors joined the game, glad for a break from their mundane duties. Soon, they were sparring, iron swords and shields against wooden swords, boards and little boy determination.

And as they laughed and jested at the boys, a young girl crept from the ditch, into the willow reeds and, lifting her skirt, waded barefoot across the creek.

****

Risa had learned through kitchen gossip which village shack housed Willow and her daughter Lola. As she knocked, she whispered a prayer for a chance to talk to Willow alone.

A sweet miniature voice sang out, "Who is it?" Then three-year-old eyes peeked out through a crack in the door.

"Hello, you must be Lola. Is your mama home?"

A voice spoke behind her, stern and suspicious. "Yes, she is. Who are you and how is it you know my daughter's name?"

Risa turned around and came face to face with Willow, the prodigal princess.

****

"You have to come to the wedding! Vala wishes it more than any other single thing for her wedding day." Lola clutched her doll, staring wide-eyed at the unexpected guest. Willow and Risa sat at a rough-cut wooden table as Risa explained the purpose of her visit. Willow wore a plain, gray village dress of coarse fabric with a stained white apron wrapped around her waist. Worry wrinkles accented her eyes as she tried to manage a whirlpool of conflicting emotions.

"You shouldn't have come here. The village is not a safe place for someone like you."

"For someone like me? You *are* someone like me, only better. Vala said you were the best."

"Vala lives in a dream world. I live in the real world. And by the way, Vala hasn't gotten around to teaching manners yet, has she?"

Risa saw she had touched a nerve so she grew quiet, hoping the moment would pass. "It is true, I have much to learn about being a princess. And I did not mean to offend. There is just so much I do not understand. Aren't you happy for Vala?"

Willow stared a long time at her hands folded in her lap. Then she looked into Risa's eyes. "Yes, I am happy for her. She is doing what is expected of a princess."

"You say that like it is a bad thing."

Willow sighed. "No, it is the right thing. What do you want to hear from me? That I failed? That I made the wrong decision? Don't you think I'm reminded of that every time..." Her voice broke, and she glanced down at Lola. Then she gathered herself. "It is much more complicated than a girl your age can possibly understand."

"I am sorry if I upset you. You owe me no explanation, and I did not come here for that. I only came because I know how much Vala still loves you, and how much it would mean to her if you attended her special day. And I thought if I came and talked to you myself..."

"Well, you thought wrong and you are wasting your time. I

don't even know how you made it to the village — warriors are guarding the bridge. How did you get past them?"

Risa then launched into the story of her little brother Jozy, and the castle gang. She described each boy with all of their wonderful quirks, and how they attacked the guards. Soon Willow was laughing at the brashness of the boys. One story led to another, and Risa saw that Willow enjoyed hearing of the castle life, reliving through Risa the memories of her early years. Then Willow asked about Risa's former life and how she had arrived at the King's castle.

Risa told her everything — of her parents, their murders, of Rinc riding into the dark village to rescue them. She told of the long ride to meet the King, of his love and his kindness. As Risa told her tale, the prodigal princess brushed away tears. An hour passed in no time, then the sound of distant trumpets interrupted their talk.

Risa jumped up from her chair. "Oh my! How long have I been here? The wedding is starting."

Willow walked her to the door and stepped outside to see her off. Risa turned to give one last plea. "Please, come with me! You have no idea how welcome you would be."

Willow hesitated, then shook her head — no. She bent down and pinched the stem of a simple daisy from her garden. "Me, go to a wedding? Dressed like this?"

"You know Vala wouldn't care, and the King... he loves you."

Willow handed Risa the daisy. "After the wedding, you give Vala this from me. And tell her that I am proud of her for doing the right thing." She then smiled a sad smile at the little visitor. "I am glad you came to see me, Risa. You listen to everything Vala tells you and study hard the *Book of Lessons*. Grow up and be a princess — and no matter how hard it might get — you wait for your prince."

Risa rushed to her and hugged her tight. "I will."

"Promise?"

"I promise."

Willow was wiping tears, "Now go, before you miss the wedding." Risa smiled, choking back emotion, then turned to go.

Willow shouted after her. "How are you going to get past the guards?"

Risa laughed. "They all know me. I make them pastries every morning. I'll get a good scolding, but they'll let me through." And with that, she disappeared around the corner of Willow's house, running down the street toward the bridge.

And a once-princess, now a prodigal, stepped into her home, closed the door, slid to the floor and wept. Lola toddled over, laid her head on her mama's lap, and joined her in a cry.

* * * * * * * * * *

Risa wiped tears as she ran. She did not want to cry in front of Willow and add to her discomfort. Though she had failed in her mission, she was still glad to have tried. She clutched the daisy — a wedding gift from one friend to another.

Risa could see the bridge a hundred yards ahead, and knew — just out of sight waiting — were the castle warriors. As she was thinking through the story she would tell them, three men stepped out between two shanties and grabbed her, one placing his hand firmly over her mouth. She was quickly dragged to a dark carriage, then whisked away westward in the opposite direction of the castle.

* * * * * * * * * *

The boys could see the prize laid out before them.

The great thing about being a little boy is that most adults never notice you. They had played pretend tag through the castle, making their way steadily toward Vala's bedroom. She was in the large ready room next door, a room full of happy maids, all laughing and talking and assisting the bride. The dress was the last thing they would need, and it was laid out on her bed where the boys had hoped it would be.

"You sure about this?" Fleabite croaked.

Jozy whirled on him, tired of being second-guessed. "This will work. No one is here. I'll be right back."

"If you get caught…"

"I'll just grab it and run, then we scatter and meet at the barn."

Jozy tip-toed forward, the others hissing encouragement. He stepped into the room and was creeping toward the dress when the firm, plump fingers of Princess Henny grabbed his ear.

"OUCH!" he bellowed. None of the boys had seen Henny seated on a stool behind the door, sewing beads onto Vala's white gloves.

"What are you doing, young man?" She heard the sound of little boys' feet running down the stairs. "Who else is out there? Why are you in Vala's room?" she asked as she pulled harder on his ear.

"Let me go! We were just playing hide and seek and I..."

"You and those other boys need to go wash your faces and get ready for the wedding." Henny slung him by his ear toward the door. "Now get! And don't let me catch any of you up here again." Jozy sprinted down the stairs, heart pounding and ear throbbing.

****

The wedding could not have been more storybook. Scores of guests in their royal finery, lords and ladies, soldiers and their sweethearts, all gathered to celebrate the wedding of Rinc and Vala. When everyone was sorted to their seats and every attendant was in place, the trumpets sounded announcing the beginning of the royal ceremony. Prince Rinc made his entrance accompanied by Angus and members of his father's royal guard. He had never looked more dashing, more nervous, more... happy. Vala was his dream come true, and now that the long awaited day had arrived, he could not stop smiling.

When the groom was settled, the trumpets announced the coming of the bride. Castle doors swung out into the courtyard, and Vala stepped out in bright white and lily lace. A daisy crown adorned her black hair, and the red blush of her cheeks was visible behind the lacy veil. There was a murmur of appreciation then a spontaneous smattering of applause as Rinc's father, Lord Callan, escorted her down the marble steps. Vala had asked him to honor her so, and you could see on his rugged, warrior face how much this moment meant to him.

Lady Ava sat in a place of honor, not far from her son. She had so often dreamed of this day and as her new daughter was escorted to her waiting son, she looked at the King and nodded her thankfulness.

The royal chaplain took charge of the ceremony as the couple clasped hands and locked eyes. They repeated their vows as directed, lost in each other. Before the chaplain's announcement made it official, Rinc respectfully asked for liberty to speak. The words were not heard by all, and that mattered not — they were meant for one.

"All my life I knew you were out there. At times I could feel your presence, sense your thoughts — even be troubled by your sadness. Vala, you were made for me and I will love you always."

Vala's eyes brimmed full. "And I you."

The chaplain took charge. "It is an honor to present to you as husband and wife, Prince Rinc and Princess Vala!" The crowd came to their feet as trumpets announced to the surrounding countryside that the marriage was official, and the King honored.

****

A lavish feast was laid, and the guests were being served when Angus noticed a stir outside the courtyard entrance where a group of warriors were conversing. One of the captains caught Angus's eye and nodded for him to join them. Angus smiled to those around him and excused himself, but his expression changed as he headed toward the soldiers. As he joined them, they stepped out of view of the courtyard.

"Prince Angus, there is a village woman down by the bridge. Tried to run past us. She's distraught, keeps insisting she needs to speak to Princess Vala."

Angus looked down the hill to where the woman was being detained. "It's just the kind of trap Ubel would set."

The captain nodded. "We thought the same. Then she mentioned Risa by name. She keeps saying Risa has been taken."

"Taken?"

"She begged me to show Princess Vala this." The captain handed Angus a simple daisy, mud spattered but freshly cut.

Angus stepped back into view of the wedding party, and caught Rinc's eye. Angus held up two fingers, then pointed to him and Vala. Rinc instantly knew something was terribly wrong.

****

Vala took one look at the crumpled daisy, then grabbed Rinc's arm. "It's Willow. When I first came here, she would always find a daisy along the path on our afternoon walks and put one in my hair. Where is she?"

Rinc pointed toward the bridge where she was being held. Vala rolled the daisy between her fingers. "What does she want?"

Angus stepped forward. "The two of you need to brace yourselves. The woman being held down there knew Risa's name — said Risa came to see her a couple of hours ago. Vala, she claims Risa has been kidnapped."

A pained cry rose in Vala. "Rinc! It has to be Ubel!"

Rinc barked orders, and soon the guards were escorting Willow up to the castle. Vala broke into a run and met them halfway, everyone else fast behind her. The two women embraced, Willow sobbing. "Willow, tell us what happened. Don't leave out a detail."

The story poured out of Willow, of Risa's visit and invitation to the wedding — of their conversation and Risa's departure.

"I gave her the daisy to give to you, then walked her to the road. She was on her way toward the bridge when I went back into the house. A few hours later, there was a knock on the door and when I opened it, the daisy was lying on the threshold with this note."

She held out a crumpled piece of parchment with a message scratched out in cryptic script.

VALA FOR THE GIRL
10 DAYS AT SUNSET
RED ROCK GORGE

"Anyone know where this place is?" Rinc asked.

Vala was ghost-white. "Yes. It's the place where Ubel lost his arm. The place where Adeen..." Her voice broke. "He's making me return to where he lost me — back to my nightmare."

****

The discussion had grown heated. Rinc was adamant that Vala stay safely in the castle, while Vala and Angus pleaded that she be allowed to go.

"Rinc, it's a ten day hard ride to get there. He'll have spies in the hills watching you come. If they don't see Vala riding with the party, then Ubel will kill Risa. I'm sorry, my brother, but there simply isn't any other way."

"The devil! There has to be another way."

Besides the three, there was Lord Callan and Willow, still distraught, blaming herself. Lord Callan allowed their emotions to run, adding nothing, staring out the window toward the west.

"Father, what do you think?"

He slowly turned, then one at a time, looked each straight in the eye. "Angus is right. Rinc, temper your anger and think like a warrior. What are our objectives?"

"To rescue Risa — and protect Vala in the process."

"What else?"

Angus stepped up, "It's time to get Vala's friend, Pem. We know that Ubel will not be at the dark fortress. Most of his men will be with him. We rescue Pem and burn his fortress."

"Good. Now you're thinking like warriors. Vala, you are the only one who knows Pem. I need you to go with Angus and three of my best men. You will take the mountain trails to Ubel's fortress. Dress as peasants, travel light but quickly."

"But what about Risa? He will kill her if I'm not with Rinc."

Lord Callan turned his gaze toward Willow, then back to Vala. "You two are about the same size."

Everyone stared at Willow. Rinc held up his hand. "I'm sorry, but I have to ask this. Can she be trusted?"

Willow wiped her tears then smoothed her simple dress. "I have made some poor decisions in my life. But that little girl came to me, and I let her down. I will do anything — anything — to help get her back safely to the castle. Lord Callan is right, Vala is the only one who knows Pem, but we all know Risa."

Rinc looked unconvinced, but Angus caught his eye. "Not long ago, little brother, I also gave you reason to doubt me. She isn't the only one who has made mistakes. I trust her. Take her with you."

One by one, each nodded agreement. Lord Callan continued, "We'll have to dye her hair black, and she will have to wear a simple veil. It will serve another purpose." He looked at Rinc. "It will convince Ubel that Vala is still a maiden." Each absorbed this without comment, knowing he was right. It would make Ubel desire her more.

"Rinc and I will accompany Willow along with ten warriors. We will come up with a plan when we get there. Vala, I need you to tell me everything you remember about the place where the exchange will take place. Is there anything else?"

The door of the room swung slowly open and a young man stepped in, dressed for battle, holding a drawn sword polished to a mirror shine. "Yes, my lord. There are two more things. First, I am going. With your permission... please. She's my sister..."

Lord Callan raised his warrior palm stopping his words. He looked hard at the young man, and saw in return perfect resolve. "Permission granted." A look of relief flooded the young man's face. "You said there were two things, my young warrior."

Twain sheathed his sword. "I listened at the door. There is a third objective." Everyone waited for him to continue.

"Ubel dies. We end this." Everyone nodded in affirmation.

Judgment Day

Ubel was shrewd in setting the meeting ten days out. There was little time to plan and long days of travel ahead. Rinc, Lord Callan, and Willow — now with dyed raven-black hair — were accompanied by nine of the King's most trusted warriors. The tenth warrior, Twain, was still weeks away from turning thirteen, but had grown in both height and strength during the previous year. Although his sword skills were exceptional for his age, he was still untested in battle.

Evenings were spent discussing strategy and reviewing all that Vala had shared with them about the road leading to Red Rock Gorge. She described a number of mountain switchbacks along the way and treacherous mountain drop-offs aplenty. It was impossible to send troops ahead to set up an ambush. They would just have to ride in and react as the situation unfolded.

As dawn broke each morning, Lord Callan would take Twain privately aside, away from the camp, and spend time with him. They spoke to no one about what transpired between them, but those in the camp could hear the clash of swords off in the distance as the two of them trained together. Rinc wondered at this, but had learned not to question his father's wisdom.

Willow always bedded away from the group. She avoided conversation and answered only direct questions. There was a sadness about her, and Rinc wanted to know more about this young woman who had influenced Vala in such an amazing way. Halfway through the ninth day of travel, they stopped briefly to rest the horses. Rinc walked over to speak to her privately.

"Willow, can we talk?"

"I do not think it would be proper. We travel together for one reason only — to save an innocent girl."

"I understand that. I do not speak to you for myself, but for Vala. She loves you dearly, and I want you to know that if there is ever anything the two of us can do to help you — because of what you mean to her — we would gladly help."

"For that I thank you both. I don't know how this will end, but, my daughter — Lola. If this ends badly..."

"You will be protected. You will return home to her."

"I hope so. I fear..." For a moment or two there was an awkward silence. She changed the subject. "The first time you came to the castle — I saw you from the village. I had left the year before, foolishly left the castle."

"I remember. The King spoke of you."

Tears coursed her cheeks. "I know you are for Vala. It is plain to see when you are together. I also know that if I had stayed, then there would have been someone for me." She brushed her tears with the sleeve of her dress. "Anyway, I can't change the past. But if something goes wrong, will you promise that Lola will be cared for? She's not to blame... Prince Rinc, she's all I have — your promise... please?"

She stared straight into his eyes with a sense of desperation that he could not refuse. "I promise."

With that she nodded, dropped her eyes and turned away as the rest of the party began mounting their horses. Nine days' travel had brought them within a day of Ubel, his troops, and Risa. Tomorrow they would meet at sunset.

****

Angus, Vala and Lord Callan's three best warriors watched the entrance of the dark fortress below. They had set a relentless pace through the mountains, desperation driving their horses forward. The castle's main gate was guarded by a handful of men, none expecting trouble, lax and casual in their duties. Still, a small force could not successfully assault the main gate.

Arne, a young warrior with extraordinary sight, spotted a second entrance along the west wall of the fortress. Just after breakfast, a maid had exited a small door that, until opened, had appeared as just part of the wall. She walked forty yards toward a sty of sows, emptied the scrap bucket, then walked to a small spring where she washed out the bucket, then filled it with water. Two guards accompanied her halfway, then stood together, laughing at some crude private joke.

Angus waited till the midday meal and saw the routine repeated. "That is our way in. After this evening's meal, we will be waiting."

They passed the next few hours looping through the woods, toward the hidden servant's entrance. There was too much open ground to cover between the pig sty and the door, so they pointed and planned, then set their ambush.

****

Anaya hated this chore most. Not that she minded the labor, or the slop, or even the smell of the pigs. It was the men who were sent to guard her. Most of the time they just made their crude remarks, but at other times.... she shuddered as she pushed away the nightmarish memories. They had been drinking, which made things worse. She opened the small door, struggled to carry the bucket, the men following as usual. She whispered a prayer as she often did, wondering why she bothered. The heavens seemed uninterested in her plight.

As she neared the pig sty, a beautiful young woman dressed in peasant attire came from the woods near the spring. She called out, begging to be fed. Anaya tried to warn her away, but the men saw the young woman, then exchanged lustful smiles. Anaya could not stand the thought of what was about to happen, so she called out.

"Run!"

One of the men backhanded Anaya, knocking her to the ground. The two then turned to see the young girl sprinting back into the woods. They cursed, then followed in hot pursuit. Moments after they entered the woods, Anaya could hear the sounds of a struggle, then total silence. The girl reappeared and motioned her toward the woods. Anaya rubbed her jaw then looked back at the dark fortress. No one had noticed what had happened, so she ran toward the girl.

****

Vala settled the hysterical young woman down. "You are safe now, but you need to help us. We don't have much time. Do you know a mute young captive by the name of Pem?"

Anaya nodded. "Yes. She has always been so kind to me."

Angus took over. "My lady, I need you to draw out a picture of the fortress. I need to know where the guards are stationed, where Ubel's quarters are, where Pem stays — everything." He smoothed the forest floor then handed Anaya a stick. "Don't leave anything out."

Again Anaya nodded, then began sketching in the soil.

****

As Lord Callan, Rinc, the veiled Willow and the ten warriors made the last, dog-leg turn toward the meeting place, they stopped and stared at what awaited. Ubel sat on a large rock near the place where his body had been crushed years before. Sitting beside him was Risa, and around them, thirty armed warriors. Twain stirred in his saddle, and Lord Callan spoke quietly.

"Easy, my young warrior. All in good time."

Lord Callan eased his horse forward, ordering the others to stay, and rode the last sixty yards to where Ubel waited.

"Lord Callan, I presume. My apologies for interrupting your

son's wedding. It was necessary. You see, he has something that belongs to me."

"And you have someone who belongs to us."

Ubel laughed. "You are all sentimental fools. Would you really trade Vala for this worthless wench? I dared not believe it when my spies brought me word that you were coming. As you can see, they also counted your warriors. My thirty to your twelve — surely you don't believe you can take the girl by force."

Lord Callan's eyes never left Ubel's. "No, I knew you would take precautions. Your reputation precedes you — you are a man who plays it... safe. A man who avoids a fair fight."

Ubel's smile faded. "What are you suggesting? A duel?"

Lord Callan's eyes rested on Ubel's ravaged arm. "Between my son and which of your men? After all..." He pointed to Ubel's stump of an arm and shrugged.

Ubel's temper flared. "Do you think that because I have lost an arm I am any less deadly? If you know my reputation, then you know that I have killed over twenty men who dared challenge me. If your son wants to keep Vala, have him fight me for his bride."

Lord Callan feigned concern. "He has only been a warrior for a few years." He furrowed his brow in thought, then continued. "But it is his fight. I will accept your proposal. He will walk Vala towards you and meet halfway. You bring the young girl. Yes, if he wants his bride he will win her, or die trying. It is the warrior's way."

Ubel smiled a wicked smile. "Say goodbye before you send him. I'll slit your pup's throat and dance in his blood."

Lord Callan stared hard, then, turned away. When he arrived, he stated the conditions and then stopped Rinc as he started to dismount. "Stay on your horse, son. I'm sending Twain."

Rinc looked at his father in disbelief. "Sending who? Father, have you lost your senses? That is Ubel! He has killed over a dozen trained warriors one on one."

"Actually, over twenty, according to him."

"Father, this is my fight!"

"No, it's not. Vala is safe and Risa is his sister. Son, I do not doubt your abilities, but I know Ubel. Trust me. When he sees that I sent a twelve-year-old to face him, then Twain will have the advantage. Ubel's worst enemy is not any of us, but his own pride."

Lord Callan then looked at Willow. "Lady, are you at peace with this plan?"

She looked at Twain, so young but so sure. "I trust your judgment, my lord. Is this our best chance to get Risa back home alive?"

Lord Callan never hesitated. "Yes, my lady."

A look of resignation shadowed her. She felt like someone had just stepped on her grave. "Then we do it."

Lord Callan walked his horse beside Twain's. He looked into his eyes and saw again perfect resolve. "Remember."

Twain nodded, then dismounted as Willow, veil in place, joined him. As they started toward Ubel, they watched him stalk confidently toward them, sword in hand, dragging Risa roughly along.

****

Angus, Vala, and the three warriors headed straight for Ubel's chambers. Anaya had told them that two of Ubel's most trusted warriors guarded the entrance, responsible for his treasures until he returned. Ubel's other guards — older men and young boys — were stationed at the front gate. The fortress was believed to be impenetrable, so Ubel's elite warriors had accompanied him to take back Vala.

Vala peeked around the corner at the two guards. Before Angus could speak, she turned and whispered, "Well, it worked once," then bolted down the street past the guards.

Angus almost swore. "I promised Rinc to keep her safe." He whispered back to his warriors. "He forgot to tell me she's half crazy."

But it did work. The guards stepped into the street as she passed, then stared after her as she smiled back at them. Angus and his men closed fast, then made short work of the guards as they tried to turn and fight. It was over in seconds.

The keys to the doors were found on one of the guards, and soon they were inside. Anaya's details of the massive fortress led them to Ubel's throne room. Wilted reeds garnished the floor, and piles of wood were stacked beside the massive fireplace. Angus pointed down the hall, then handed Vala the keys.

"You go get Pem and whoever else he has locked up. Then meet me back here. You two, go with her. Arne and I will prepare to torch this place. Now hurry!"

Vala led the two men down the hall, calling Pem's name. She tried to harness her emotions, but tears flowed as she cried out. A woman's voice answered at the end of the hall from behind a locked door. Vala could not see the key hole through her tears so one of the warriors unlocked the door instead. Inside, huddled together, were seven young women, then Pem broke from the group toward her.

Their embrace was sweet, their tears unrestrained as both were finally reunited. The other women were frightened by the drawn swords of the warriors, so Vala explained they were there to rescue them. The other six women were ushered through the door down the hall, but Pem grabbed Vala and began pulling her the opposite way.

"Pem, we have to go!" Pem pulled Vala toward another locked door, pointing and pleading with her eyes. Vala cried out to the warrior who had the keys. A few seconds later, he swung the door open, and there, standing in the middle of the room, was a little sugar-and-spice toddler — same Pem eyes; same Pem sad smile. She scampered to Pem and buried her face in her skirts. Vala reached down and touched the child's golden locks, then looked at Pem.

"Your daughter?" Pem smiled and nodded. Vala smiled back, then hugged them both. "Oh, Pem. She's beautiful!" The small girl narrowed her eyes, stuck out her chin and asked, "Who are you? And why is my Mommy crying?"

Vala knelt in front of the little girl. "I'm your mommy's friend. We've come to take you both to a better place — a safe place." And with that, Pem plucked up her daughter, then followed Vala as they ran back to the throne room where fires were being lit.

As they arrived, Angus looked up at the young woman carrying the child. Pem stopped and their eyes locked, smoke and flames all around. Then Pem smiled and, for the first time ever, it wasn't a sad smile. Vala noticed Angus staring, taking in Pem's blue eyes, high cheekbones, wide mouth and blonde hair — the two, frozen in time, as the fire spread around them. Vala smiled, shaking her head, then shouted, "Angus, we need to go... now!"

Angus broke from his trance, then he and the three warriors, Vala, Pem and her daughter, and the other six young captives headed out of the fortress and past the pig sty where Anaya waited. They slipped into the forest as the smoke began to billow behind them.

As they went, Angus kept glancing back, drawn to the young woman who would never speak, but all the same seemed to be calling.

****

Ten paces from halfway, Ubel stopped, measuring the lad who met him. He shoved Risa to the ground, as she called out Twain's name. Twain glanced at her then said in a calm voice, "Stay on the ground, Risa." Then he locked eyes with Ubel, and closed the distance to three paces. Willow stayed put.

Ubel spat words at Twain. "You are not Lord Callan's son. Why, you are a mere child!"

"Prince Rinc saw no need to bother himself with the likes of you. I am Twain. I come in the name of the King, to execute his justice." Twain drew his sword, his eyes mocking Ubel.

Willow then spoke as she removed her veil. "And I am not Vala. You are a pig — your eyes are not worthy to look upon her. I came in Vala's place so that I can describe to her later how a mere boy killed the mighty Ubel. I came to witness your death."

Ubel now was shaking with rage, but before he could speak, Twain did the unthinkable. He spat on the ground then turned his back with disdain upon Ubel.

Ubel snapped. Risa screamed as Ubel roared, closed the distance, raised his sword, then brought it down in a savage arc — unleashing all his strength into the killing stroke.

What Ubel failed to notice was that when Twain turned his back, he also lifted his sword in front of him watching Ubel's reflection in its mirrored surface. This is what Lord Callan had taught him. They had practiced this a hundred times in the last week, until he mastered the move and perfected the killing thrust. As Ubel's blade descended,

Twain used his lightning speed to twist inside Ubel's swing, avoiding the blade, while thrusting his own sword straight at Ubel's face. The tip pierced Ubel's right eye then slashed out the back of his head. The dark lord convulsed as his roar turned into a death scream. Time stood still, then Ubel's body fell backward onto the dusty road.

Lord Callan had directed his men to charge as soon as Ubel attacked. Ubel's troops were so stunned at the defeat of their lord by a mere boy, that they hesitated. By the time they reacted, Lord Callan's warriors had formed a shield wall, Rinc anchoring the middle, Willow, Risa and Twain safe behind it. Still, they were outnumbered thirty to twelve.

Ubel's troops advanced slowly, forming their own shield wall. Their leader looked determined to avenge the death of their lord. Lord Callan spoke out of the shield wall and addressed the dark warriors. "Your lord is dead. He was defeated by a boy. If you wish to avenge your lord, then we will fight. You may win, but I promise, many of you will die."

The warriors looked undaunted. Lord Callan continued, "My eldest son has led an assault on Ubel's fortress. By now, they have won, and your lord's chambers are being torched." This caused a stir among the dark warriors. Several glanced behind them, and far off across the valley, they could see dark smoke rising.

"You can stay and fight. But what about your lord's gold and silver? What of his treasures? Do you trust those left behind to share with you the plunder? How generous was your lord when he was alive? Generous enough to die for?"

The men murmured amongst themselves until their greed won out. They walked back to their horses and soon were racing back toward the inflamed fortress.

As they left, Risa embraced Twain as she sobbed tears of relief. Lord Callan watched the reunion, then caught Twain's eye and nodded his respect. Twain nodded back as he held his sister.

Willow suddenly sat down in the middle of the road, overcome by what had just happened. Risa broke from Twain, raced to her, calling her name. They embraced and the tears flowed. "What did they do to your hair? At first, I thought you were Vala."

Willow fingered her hair and smiled. "Yes, I guess it worked."

Risa looked at her with admiration. "Willow, that was the bravest thing I have ever seen. Vala will be so proud of you."

Rinc came over and knelt beside them. Willow looked at him, still shaking. "I was convinced that I would die today. I should have, for the things I've done. Why am I still alive?"

Rinc smiled. "Maybe it takes more courage to live than it does to die. There are unfinished purposes for your life. You have a daughter to raise, and by now she is missing her mama." He reached for her hand and helped her to her feet. "So, let's get mounted up...

"It's time to go back to the castle."

****

There is nothing quite like coming home.

Lord Callan led his warriors triumphantly up to the castle, Twain riding beside him, Risa seated behind holding on to her brother's waist. A cheer rose from the ramparts that shook the countryside.

Pem and Phemie found a home in the King's castle — a safe place at last. Angus was smitten by Pem, and Phemie latched on to him on the ride back like she already knew something the two of them were still figuring out. Angus knew it would take time, that Pem would need to heal. There was no better place for that than in the castle.

Willow asked to be dropped off at her village shack. She had been quiet on the journey back — a peaceful quiet. A few hours later, after picking up Lola from a friend's care, the two crossed the bridge and climbed up the hill towards the castle. The King met them halfway — sweet embrace, joyful tears, and whispered words. Then, together, they walked to the castle.

The prodigal princess was home.

As for Rinc and Vala, they didn't stay long at the castle. As the two newlyweds rode away, their happiness spilled out in laughter, echoing through the hills and valleys, and then to the skies above. They didn't tell anyone where they were going and were not seen again for several weeks.

Other Books by the Author

Seven Royal Laws of Courtship
The Teenage Years of Jesus Christ
The Childhood Years of Jesus Christ
The 21 Tenets of Biblical Femininity
The 21 Tenets of Biblical Masculinity
Is Your Youth Group Dead or Alive?
Mountain Lessons
Grace Will Lead Me Home
104 Teen Bible Lessons
Did God Put a Book Inside of You?

Stay in the Castle Series

Stay in the Castle
The Warrior Prince
The Chosen One
The Prodigals

The Teenager's Guide Series

A Teenager's Guide to Character, Success, & Happiness
A Teenager's Guide to the Invisible Creation
A Teenager's Guide to Healthy Relationships

Ultimate Goal Publications

Order by phone or online
(812) 665-4375
www.stayinthecastle.com